C.L.U.T.Z.

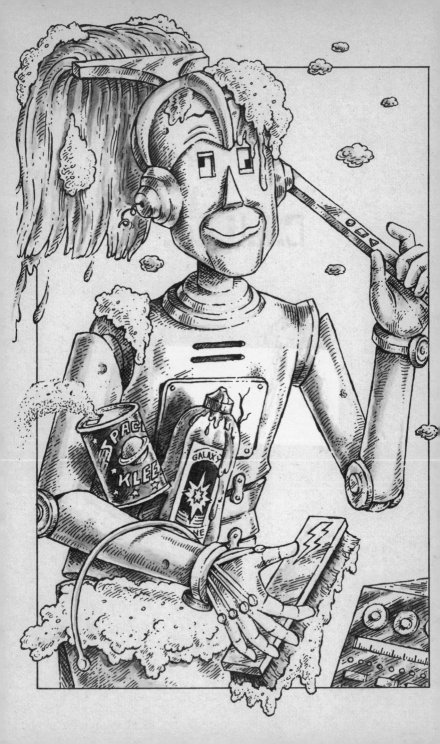

Weekly Reader Books presents

C.L.U.T.Z.

MARILYN Z. WILKES

pictures by Larry Ross

The Dial Press / New York

ACKNOWLEDGMENTS

Sincere thanks to Alan Wilson,
Research Staff Member of IBM's Watson Laboratory,
for reading the manuscript of *C.L.U.T.Z.*
with a scientist's eye.

Published by
The Dial Press
1 Dag Hammarskjold Plaza
New York, New York 10017

Library of Congress Cataloging in Publication Data
Wilkes, Marilyn / C.L.U.T.Z.
Summary / Eleven-year-old Rodney makes a new friend
when a broken-down robot with an almost human
personality comes to work for his family.
[1. Science fiction. 2. Robots—Fiction]
I. Ross, Larry, 1943–   ill. II. Title. III. Title: C.L.U.T.Z.
PZ7.W64839Clu [Fic] 81–68786 AACR2
ISBN 0–8037–1157–3 / ISBN 0–8037–1158–1 (lib. bdg.)

*For Ben, who introduced me
to science fiction,
And Josh, my chief critic
and moral support.*

C.L.U.T.Z.

It was Saturday morning, Rodney Pentax's favorite time of the week. He ambled into the leisure room and pressed a button on the console in the middle of the floor. Instantly the *Daily Telecom* lit up across the leisure room wall, bringing with it "All the News That's Fit to Transmit." Still in his sleepsuit, Rodney curled up on a float-a-lounge and bit into his third breakfast bar. He tossed a piece to the large fuzzy pink *Muttus* lying on the floor near his feet. Aurora Borealis caught it neatly in her mouth and wagged her tail.

"You're welcome," said Rodney. He switched the telecom to Fast Forward. He couldn't wait to see the sports section and the outcome of the moonball playoffs. He had a two-credit bet with Tyler Khan, his friend in Tower 7 of the John Glenn Living Complex, that the United Federation of North America would beat the Martian Colonials for the third time in a row.

Rodney viewed the home report. Chief Skycop Adler reported an increase in high-atmospheric traffic accidents in the Northeast Sector. Helijet speed limits were being reduced to subsonic levels over all population zones. The stock market was up, due to the new asteroid mining operations near Jupiter. And McDonald's Interstellar announced a new minicapsule that, with the addition of water, became a Quarter-Kilo with Cheese.

At last the sports news appeared. Earth's United Federation of North America had done it again! Rodney grinned. Two credits would buy a Planetoids game module for his pocket computer. He couldn't wait to call Tyler. Maybe they could watch the replay of the game on holovision together. Moonball was their favorite sport.

The classified ads came on. Rodney reached over

to shut off the telecom, but something caught his eye:

ROBOT WANTED, USED, HOUSEHOLD DUTIES. MUST BE EFFICIENT, GOOD WITH CHILDREN, GOOD COOK. LEASE OR BUY. VID. 212-8864-7098P.

"Hey, Aurora, that's *our* video number! Come on!" Rodney jumped up and ran down the hall to his parents' room.

"Mom, Dad," he said, "was that our ad on the telecom? Are we really getting a robot?"

"Maybe," said Mr. Pentax from the bathroom. He rinsed off his ultrasonic toothbrush and vac-dried his hands and face. "If we can afford it, of course."

Mrs. Pentax was unwrapping a package of disposa-shorts for her husband. "It's partly because of you, dear," she said. "Since Grandma Deedee moved away last month, you've had to be on your own far too much."

"I'm old enough to take of care of myself," said Rodney. "And I've got Aurora." Aurora Borealis barked in agreement.

"You're only eleven annums old," said Mrs. Pentax, "and a *Muttus primaverus* is just a dog. Even one as intelligent and devoted as Aurora. Besides, with both of us working all day, your father and I need help taking care of the living unit and doing the cooking. Things haven't been run very well around here lately."

"They haven't been run at all!" said Arthur Pentax, fastening the disposa-shorts around his middle. "I haven't had a decent meal since your grandmother ran off to the Satellite for Seniors with that crazy new husband of hers. I've even gotten to like Martian cooking, if you can believe it."

Rodney's father worked for the Asteroid Candy Company as a Nutri-Sweets salesman, servicing the satellites and colonies from Earth to Mars. It meant he was away a lot. Of course, when he came home, he always brought plenty of Nutri-Sweets, the high-protein vitamin and mineral treat— "The round candy bar that's a square meal."

A buzzer buzzed and the light on the video-phone went on. "I'll bet that's Tyler," said Rodney. Mr. Pentax touched a button on the unit next to his bed.

"Good morning, sir!" said a dark-haired smily-faced man from the videoscreen. "Is this the party that's looking for a good buy on a robot, may I ask?"

"Buy or lease," said Mr. Pentax, "depending on the cost. Do you have one?"

"One? My dear sir," said the face, "I represent Ralph's Robots Interplanetary. We have forty-eight showrooms around the globe, ten on Luna, five on Mars, and four coming soon on Ganymede, the third moon of Jupiter. We have more than *one thousand* different robots for your inspection. 'Whatever your need, we've a robot for the deed' at Ralph's. Why don't I show you a few in our domestic line?"

"Well, all right," said Mr. Pentax. "But nothing too—"

A sleek, silvery image with glowing red eyes filled the videoscreen. It was wearing a formal black metal jumpsuit and white gloves.

"Here you are," said the salesman briskly. "Our top-of-the-line Model A85-B, the Butler-Did-It. And what did he do? you may ask. Why, everything, my good man, everything! The A85-B is a meticulous housekeeper and expert cook in every

known cuisine. He is programmed for advanced degrees in child psychology and nuclear medicine and makes all his own clothes. His syncro-meshed brain can anticipate your every domestic need—a perfect robot for the perfect home. And the cost for this marvel of modern technology is a mere 65,000 credits, easy financing available. Or, if you wish, only 8,000 credits per annum on a ten-annum lease."

Mr. Pentax gulped. "He's very impressive, but that's a bit more than we had intended to spend. . . ."

The salesman looked understanding. "I see," he said. "Then perhaps our Model C87-N, the Nanny," he suggested. "She might be more what you had in mind.

The screen displayed a shiny gold-colored robot with a graceful female form dressed neatly in a white plastoid nurse's cap and sensible shoes.

"This robot's specialties include the ability to avoid waxy buildup, one hundred ways with casseroles, and an extensive repertoire of games and songs for the very young. A steal at 45,000 credits, or 6,900 per annum."

"I don't think so," said Mr. Pentax. "I hate

casseroles, and that's still pretty expensive. Don't you have anything in the 'slightly used' department? We did specify used, you know.

"Well," said the salesman with sudden coolness, "we don't really get into that sort of thing anymore. We find that most old robots are fit only for scrap or recycling after their owners are finished with them.

"However, we did take in this model, R-99. It's five annums old, used by a little old lady only on alternate Tuesdays, when her other robot was being recharged." A rusty, boxlike object on wheels squeaked into view. "It has a built-in dry-cleaning plant, and it's a whiz with freeze-dried insta-meals. I can let you have it for 18,000 credits, no lease, and I don't want to know about it once it's yours."

"We'll have to talk it over," said Mr. Pentax. "Thank you very much." He flipped off the videoscreen.

"Eighteen thousand credits for that piece of junk!" said Mrs. Pentax. "He has a lot of nerve."

Rodney was excited. "Can't we go see the rest of his robots?" he asked. "He's got a thousand of them. There's bound to be one we like. I thought that fancy black one was spacy. I'll bet it can even play moonball."

"I don't know," said Mrs. Pentax. "They're all so expensive. We may have to think of some other solution to our problem."

"We've got to do something," grumbled Mr. Pentax. "I can't face one more insta-meal or another day of this disposable underwear. It itches."

Aurora sat up on the foot of the bed and growled.

"What is it, girl?" asked Rodney.

The dog trotted down the hall to the front door and barked ferociously.

"She hears somebody," said Rodney. "She always hears them before they ring the bell."

The doorbell rang. With her large black nose Aurora pressed a button on the doorframe. The door slid open and Aurora resumed her barking much to the dismay of the creature standing outside.

It was a robot. He seemed much the worse for wear. His finish, which Rodney supposed had been a brass alloy of some kind, was badly oxidized. And there was something cock-eyed about the way his joints were fastened together, so that he looked as if he might topple over at any moment.

Most disconcerting, though, was the small coiled spring that sprouted from one shell-like ear. It *boing*ed up and down whenever he moved his head. Rodney had an uncontrollable urge to push it back into the metal cranium where it belonged.

Instead, he said, "Hello. Who are you?"

The robot gave him a friendly glassy-eyed smile.

"Hel-lo," he said. "I am a Combined Level Unit/Type Z." He scratched stiffly at one dented leg and peered at Aurora.

"Dogs give me hives."

·2·

Aurora continued to growl.

"Aurora! Cut it out!" said Rodney. "I don't know what's gotten into her. She usually likes—uh—everybody."

"Oh, that's all right," the robot assured him. "Mechanical marvels such as myself are often hard for mere dumb animals to comprehend." Aurora barked indignantly. The robot took a step backward and cocked his head. "Is it safe to enter?" he asked.

"Oh, sure," said Rodney. The robot raised one

foot, tripped, and half-staggered, half-fell across the threshold. Rodney caught him by the elbow.

"Nasty step you've got there," said the robot, straightening his breastplate.

"Rodney, what is all that clattering?" asked Mrs. Pentax.

The robot bowed crookedly. "Madam, I am a Combined Level Unit/Type Z," he announced. Rodney watched the tiny coiled spring bounce in his ear. "I have come in response to your ad."

Mr. Pentax came down the hall, zipping the front of his at-home suit. "How did you get here?" he asked. "Robots don't just wander in alone from nowhere."

"Sir," said the robot, his voice suddenly trembling. "I am not from nowhere. But that is where I'm going, unless— Oh, sir, madam, I have come here to apply for—to *beg* for—the job of domestic robot in your lovely abode."

"Here? Well, I don't know," said Mrs. Pentax, startled. "We can't say, just like that. What about your owners? How do we know you aren't lost or suffering from a memory lapse or a loose screw or something?" She eyed suspiciously the spring protruding from his ear.

"Let me assure you," said the robot, "that all my screws are perfectly tight." He shook his head to illustrate. The spring wobbled madly.

"But I *am* suffering—terribly," the robot continued. "The truth is, I no longer have a home or owners. They threw me out the way you would throw out an old broken-down—machine."

Mr. Pentax opened his mouth to say something, but Mrs. Pentax quickly nudged him with her elbow.

"My owners—my former owners—bought a new robot last week. A Butler Something-or-Other, with a fancy black suit and white gloves. Can you believe a robot with *gloves*? It's pretentious, really.

"Of course, he's Mr. Perfect, always cleaning and straightening everything. And whenever my back was turned, he would pick *me* up and dump me on the trash conveyor. The first few times my owners thought it was terribly funny. Then they decided that Mr. Black Suit was right. He was so efficient that they didn't need me anymore. He could do a day's work in half a day and still have time to play moonball with the robots down the hall before dinner."

"What did I tell you?" Rodney said to his parents.

"So this morning, when I was dumped on the trash conveyor along with the breakfast dishes, Mrs. Floton—that's my former owner—told Mr. Floton to leave me and let the Salvation Forces have me for scrap. After twelve annums of faithful service! I was so devastated that I just let myself be carried off. After all, it was the will of the humans I served, and I had to do everything they desired, even if it meant the end of me. A robot is created solely to serve humans, you know.

"And so I was on the way to my doom at the recycling plant when your telecom ad surfaced in my memory banks. Perhaps, I thought, here is an even better chance to serve! The Flotons will be happy, thinking I have been recycled—which in a way I have been—and now I can provide a second family with the assistance they need. Oh, lucky me!

"So I struggled out from under a pile of disposed disposables and went looking for your address in the city databanks. At last I stumbled across it, and here I am." He stopped to scratch his arm. Aurora muttered under her breath.

"You stumbled across us, all right," said

Rodney, smiling. He was fascinated by the robot. He seemed like such a nice—machine? creature? being? Rodney wasn't sure how to think of him. He hadn't known robots could have so much personality. Almost like a real person. Imagine allowing him to be thrown out like a bag of garbage! It was cruel!

"Can he stay, Mom, Dad? Please? He hasn't got anywhere else to go, and we need a robot."

"We'll have to discuss it, Rodney," said Mrs. Pentax.

"Then let's discuss it," said Rodney. "My discussion counts, too, doesn't it, since I'm one of the reasons we're getting a robot? I like this robot—a lot. He's nice, and friendly, and I'll bet he can cook and clean. And he won't cost us a single credit. You can't beat that. Right, Dad?"

"Rodney has a point, Lyra," said Mr. Pentax. "The price is right. And he appears to be a good chap. A little odd and beat-up, perhaps, but sincere. Seems a waste to let him end up as scrap metal when he could be of use to us."

"I'm not sure he would be," said Mrs. Pentax. "How do you know he's competent? He looks so—dubious. I don't know about you, Arthur, but I can't go off to F.O.R.K. for a whole day and leave just anybody—I mean, anything—in charge of our home and our son. There's no end to what could happen. At least if we bought a new robot, we would know it was reliable. We would have a guarantee."

"Dear lady," said the robot, "I am extremely reliable. I will give you my own guarantee. I will serve you as faithfully as I know how, and if you are not completely satisfied, I will go to my fate without a murmur."

"Why don't we call up his old owners?" suggested Rodney. "They can tell us what kind of job he did."

"Oh, you couldn't do that!" said the robot. "They think I'm—deceased." He shuddered.

"We can tell them we're thinking of buying a used robot just like you," said Rodney. "And we want to know whether they recommend it or not. It might convince my parents to let you stay."

"In that case," said the robot, "the number is 201-5578-2250F."

They went into the leisure room. Mr. Pentax punched the number into the videophone. After a moment a velvety voice answered, "Floton residence." A familiar black-and-silver image filled the screen.

"May I speak to Mr. or Mrs. Floton," said Mr. Pentax.

"I am sorry," hummed the velvet voice. "The Flotons are away on an extended trip while their living quarters are being remodeled. The required work was so extensive that they could not remain here in comfort while it was being carried out. In their absence I am in charge. May I ask who is calling? I know they will be happy to speak with you upon their return."

"Oh. No, never mind," said Mr. Pentax. "That won't be necessary."

"It has been my pleasure to serve you," hummed the voice. Two red eyes glowed briefly. Then the picture on the videophone went dark.

"That was You-Know-Who," said the robot.

"He gave me the creeps," said Rodney.

"He looked extremely efficient to me," said Mrs. Pentax. "He seemed to take his job very seriously."

"Oh, I would, too, madam," said the robot. "I am both earnest and sincere. I am programmed for even greater loyalty than the average family dog."

Aurora lunged for a metal ankle. Rodney grabbed her.

"In fact," the robot continued, "I am programmed with all the human virtues: honesty, courage, love, kindness, compassion. Intelligence, too." He looked down modestly. "I am no dummy, as it were."

"Then why did the Flotons replace you?" asked Mrs. Pentax. "How did you fail to meet their needs?"

"Dear lady, you have every right to ask," replied the robot. "I must explain.

"I am a Combined Level Unit/Type Z, of a class introduced about fifty annums ago. We revolutionized robot science. For the first time, robots combined more than one level of accomplishment. Not only did we have logical-intellectual and mechanical skills, but we also incorporated all the positive emotions found in humans."

"Why was that so important?" asked Mr. Pentax.

"Because it made us more acceptable to the humans who needed us," answered the robot. "Robots were already used widely in factories and

mines, in difficult and dangerous jobs. They could withstand heat and cold, radiation, and atmospheres unhealthy to humans. But there was so much more they could do.

"However, when humans were encouraged to use robots in their daily lives, the idea met with resistance. Robots were so cold, so emotionless. They gave people, as you so rightly said, young man, the creeps.

"Now, here was a class of robots who could be friendly, loving, good-humored. The resistance to using such beings in the home, with children, the sick, and the elderly, was overcome. At last humans could benefit truly from the fruits of their own technology!"

"Where do you fit into all this?" asked Mr. Pentax.

"I was part of that first experimental group, Type Z. We were pioneers in the field. Of course, being the first, we had our share of small flaws. Emotions and perfect function do not go hand in hand, you know."

"What kinds of flaws?" asked Mrs. Pentax suspiciously.

"Only minor ones," said the robot. "But some

improvements were made. The next group, Type Y, was a bit steadier under pressure. Type X could cry 'real' tears, and so on.

"The series reached its peak with Type A— C.L.U.T.A. It was a technological triumph, with a female form and personality." He sighed with remembrance.

"Of course, changes still continue to be made, as tastes and needs dictate. That robot the Flotons bought is the latest in functional perfection. But its personality mode has been cut back severely in order to make room on its brain chips for so many skills. It has all the charm of a ball bearing."

"Hmmm," said Mr. Pentax. "If what you say is true—"

"I assure you it is, sir," said the robot. "I am technologically incapable of lying."

"In that case," said Mr. Pentax, "we might as well give you a try. A week, perhaps. What do you think, Lyra? A week can't hurt. We can decide then."

"I'm not totally convinced," said Mrs. Pentax. "But I suppose it would be all right, on a trial basis only."

"Yippee!" yelled Rodney. "You're staying!" He

clapped the startled robot on the back. "Come on, Type Z. I'll show you around. You come, too, Aurora." But Aurora cast a reproachful glance at Rodney and flounced out of the room.

"Just a minute, uh, Type Z," said Arthur Pentax.

"Yes, master?" said the robot with his most ingratiating smile.

"Don't you have a real name, something a little less—formal?"

"I am sometimes called by my acronym," said the robot.

"Your what?" asked Rodney's father.

"The first letters of my full name—C.L.U.T.Z. Clutz." The robot turned to smile at Rodney, bumped into a float-a-lounge, and sent it sailing across the room.

"Oops," he said, tottering after the chair and replacing it where it belonged.

Rodney laughed. "Come on, Clutz," he said. He put his arm around the robot's shoulders and guided him down the hall.

Rodney flopped down on his bed. "Sit here next to me so we can talk," he said to Clutz. "There's so much I want to know about you."

Aurora jumped up on the bed and bared her teeth at the robot.

"Oh, thank you, Master Rodney," said Clutz, scratching his left wrist. "I'll just try this chair, if you don't mind."

"Of course I don't mind," said Rodney. "This is your home now, too. At least I hope it will be your home."

"Oh, I do, too," said Clutz. He gazed warmly at Rodney. "Nothing could make me happier. I feel that I've come to the right place."

Aurora sprawled on the bed and closed one eye. The other was fastened on Clutz. Rodney scratched her behind the ear. "Things will work out," he said. "We'll *make* them work out. Now, tell me. What's it like to be a robot?"

Thirty minutes later Clutz consulted the chronometer built into his left wrist. "I should be getting busy," he said. "That is why I'm here, after all." Rodney and Aurora followed him into the leisure room.

There was so much to do. Several days newsfilms were scattered on the floor, along with the electronic jigsaw puzzles Rodney had forgotten to put away. There was dust on the console and a pile of Nutri-Sweets wrappers under a float-a-lounge.

"I will clean the living unit now," Clutz announced to Mr. and Mrs. Pentax. "I will straighten each room, remove the dust, wash the floors, clean the baths, wash the windows, and vacuum the upholstery. A mere morning's work."

The Pentaxes were impressed.

Laden with cleaning supplies, Clutz staggered down the hall to begin. For half an hour, there were sounds of great activity. Then, suddenly, silence. Rodney went to investigate.

"Hey, Clutz," he called. "Where are you?"

"In here, Rodney," a muffled voice answered. Rodney looked in the bathroom. There was the robot, hanging over the edge of the sunken whirlpool tub, his head a few centimeters from the swirling water.

"What are you doing?" asked Rodney. "Taking a bath?"

"Oh, Rodney, of course not," said Clutz. "I was cleaning the tub and bent over to turn on the whirlpool spray. I seem to have thrown my back out. I am prone to back trouble. It's the fifth vertebearing again, I think. Could you please help me up?"

Rodney fastened his arms around the robot's breastplate and heaved upward. There was a sharp *ping*.

"Aah," said Clutz. "That did it." He stood up and wriggled his shoulders tentatively. "Thank goodness. The last time this happened, I had to go into the hospital for repairs. Let me tell you, a robot hospital is a dreadful place. Not a private cubicle anywhere. And they poke around your insides until you feel worse than when you came in."

"I'm afraid you'll end up in a worse place than a robot hospital if you don't do a good job here," said Rodney.

"Don't remind me," said Clutz. He picked up a disposa-mop and headed for the leisure room.

"First job, dust removal," he announced. He went to the House-Kleen control panel on the wall and pressed a couple of buttons. There was a whirring noise. Soon all the air in the living unit was circulating toward small grills near the ceiling, filtering out dust and recirculating clean air.

"Now the vacuuming," said Clutz. "I *do* love to vacuum." He pulled the nozzle of the vacuum hose out of the panel and ran it around the floors and furniture. There was a series of clanks and chinks as the machine sucked up dirt, Nutri-Sweets wrappers, a writing stylus, a handful of credit disks, and Aurora's new plasti-chew toy. She began to bark.

Dust balls swirled. They made Clutz sneeze.

"Aaaa*shoo*!!" The spring in his ear bounced violently. He snorted and snuffled and squeaked. The sounds echoed through his metallic sinuses.

"AA—AAAH—AAA*SHOOOO*!!"

Rodney jumped up as Clutz staggered blindly across the room, straight toward Mr. Pentax's audio center. Rodney's father threw himself over the delicate equipment in an effort to protect it. Too late. Cassette tubes flew everywhere. Storage racks clattered to the floor. Clutz sank, gasping, into a float-a-lounge.

Rodney hurried to pick everything up. "He can't help being allergic," he said to his father.

"An allergic robot," said Mr. Pentax. "No family should be without one."

Rodney held Clutz's arm as the robot dragged himself into the kitchen, wheezing and croaking, and pressed the button on the cold-water tap. Then he slid open his breastplate and removed a fiberplast air filter. He washed and dried the filter carefully, replaced it in the slot in his chest, and slid the breastplate closed.

"That's better," he said with a sigh.

"You don't really breathe through that thing, do you?" asked Rodney.

"I don't require oxygen as you do," said Clutz, clearing his throat. "But I do take in air as I talk and move about. And when my filter gets dirty, I start to cough and wheeze. It still feels a bit scratchy in there. What I really need is a spray or two of silicone."

"I'll see if we have some," said Rodney.

By dinnertime Clutz was feeling much better and insisted on making dinner himself. It was delicious.

"Just like Mother used to make," said Mr. Pentax happily. As a matter of fact, Rodney's grandmother *had* made the protosoy Stroganoff and algae puffs. Clutz had found them in the cryobin and simply popped them into the micro-sonic unit to cook.

For dessert there was chocofreez, Rodney's favorite. There was chocofreez every week at the Pentaxes'. Rodney had a standing order at F.O.R.K., the food distribution center where his mother worked.

After dinner Clutz cleared the table and cleaned up while the Pentaxes enjoyed a second cup of stimu-tea.

"This really is very pleasant," said Mrs. Pentax,

leaning back in her chair. "It's nice not to have to throw out the dishes myself for a change."

Rodney beamed. "I'll go see if there's any more dessert," he said, heading for the kitchen to keep Clutz company. Aurora followed glumly.

The next morning, while Mrs. Pentax instructed Clutz about breakfast, Rodney got on the videophone. A few minutes later the doorbell rang. Aurora ran over and pressed the Open button with her nose.

It was Tyler. He had brought Danno and Jonni Cruse from Tower 4.

"Hey, Aurora," said Tyler. "Gimme a greet!" Aurora patted his outstretched hand with her right paw.

"Hey, Pentax," he called. "Where is it?"

"Yeah, *take me to your robot*," said Danno, marching in, stiff-legged.

"He's in the kitchen," said Rodney. "Come on and meet him."

"I am delighted to know you all," said Clutz with a crooked bow. "Any friends of Master Rodney's are my friends, too." He smiled his glassy-eyed smile.

"What's wrong with his ear?" asked Jonni.

"He looks pretty beat-up to me," said Danno.

"I think he's supersonic," said Tyler.

"Never mind how he looks. He's more fun than anything," said Rodney. "You'll see."

They all ran down the hall to Rodney's room.

"Can we see how he works?"

"How does he talk and smile like that?"

"Where did you get him?"

"Can he do your homework?"

"Gentlemen!" cried Clutz. "I will answer your questions and amuse you in any way I can. I am programmed to tell witty stories, sing the Top Forty for the year 2100, and play chess, Planetary Monopoly, and the Game of Space."

"How about moonball?" asked Danno. "Some robots can play it."

"Yeah," said Jonni. "Those Butler types. They can do anything."

"So can Clutz," said Rodney. "He's as good as any robot. He could learn to play moonball if I taught him. Maybe I will."

Moonball! That night, lying in bed, listening to Aurora snore softly at his feet, Rodney could think of nothing else. Maybe he *could* teach Clutz to play. What a team they'd make! With Aurora as goalie, himself as forward, and Clutz as fullback. . . . *The giant white ball sailed through the one-sixth gravity as they advanced on the opponent's goal. . . . Upward they sailed in unison. . . . Clutz shoved the ball toward him. . . . He grasped it with outstretched arms. . . . He threw. . . . A score! . . . The crowd went wild!* Rodney smiled and closed his eyes.

Rodney awoke from a deep sleep. In his dream he and Clutz were about to receive the Olympic moonball medal. Reluctantly he opened his eyes. Something was wrong. What was that horrible smell?

Aurora whined and snuffled at the foot of the bed. The chronometer set into the wall above his computer console read 7:01:34. On a school day Rodney never got up before 8:00:00. What a way to start the week.

Rodney pulled himself out of bed and went to find out where the smell was coming from. Aurora rolled over and tunneled under the heat layer, grumbling at having been disturbed.

"Good morning, Master Rodney," Clutz called

out cheerily from the food-preparation center of the kitchen. Puffs of oily smoke floated around his head. "Breakfast is ready."

"Clutz," said Rodney, eyeing the smoke with alarm. "How can you burn bacon that's already cooked?"

"Not burned, Master Rodney," insisted Clutz, placing three charred, rigid strips on Rodney's plate. "Just brown. I wanted it to be nice and hot for you."

"I'm sure it is," said Rodney quickly. "Just the way I like it. What is there to go with the, uh, bacon? Any lunabird eggs? Proto-bagels? Yeast cakes and syrup?"

"Lunabird eggs, coming up," sang Clutz. He dumped two semicooked green lumps onto Rodney's plate. Rodney stared at them. Quivering, they stared back.

"Actually, Clutz, if I could just have some citro juice—I'm not too hungry this morning. Where are Mom and Dad?"

"Your father left quite early this morning for Beta Colony. He will return tomorrow. Your mother just left—reluctantly, I think—for her day's employment at F.O.R.K. She seemed afraid

to leave me in charge. I don't know what she was expecting—burned bacon and underdone eggs, I suppose."

"I suppose," said Rodney, looking down at his plate.

"Well," said Clutz, "we'll show her, won't we?"

"The eggs?" asked Rodney with alarm.

"No, no. We'll show her that I can manage the household and take care of you," said Clutz. "You know, Rodney"—he fixed his earnest, glassy stare upon Rodney's face—"I love being part of this family already. It's nothing like my last family. I was just a *thing* to them, like the dust vacuum or the microsonic food processor.

"I know—that's all I am, really, a thing. But I have feelings, too. I am *programmed* to have feelings, whether I want them or not. And it's so much nicer when those feelings can be happy ones. Do you understand what I mean?" His gaze was luminous.

"Sure I do, Clutz," said Rodney. "We like you, too. In fact, I think you're the greatest thing that ever happened around here. And—thanks for breakfast. It was terrific."

"Why, thank you, Rodney. I'm happy that I

was able to please you." Smiling, he reached for Rodney's dishes. His hand struck the plate and sent it crashing to the floor. He walked awkwardly around a chair, clucking to himself and stepping on a round, gelatinous lunabird egg. It squished under his foot, but he was unaware.

Rodney fled from the kitchen.

School didn't start for ten more minutes. As usual everybody was hanging around in front of the EdSec MidSchool, waiting until the last minute to go inside.

"Man, it's the life," Taurus Johnson was saying. "Since we got our robot, nobody at our place does a thing anymore. Old Slick does it all."

"Yeah," said his brother, Angus. "No more chores for us! Me and Taurus, we spend all our time playing moonball and just hanging out."

"You're so lucky," said Jonni. "I wish our folks would get a robot."

"Hey, Pentax," said Taurus. "Haven't you got a robot? Or was that a two-legged hat rack I saw you with yesterday? I haven't seen that much old metal since the last space salvage mission got back."

Angus laughed. Aurora growled. She didn't like the Johnson brothers. They had chased her all the way up to Level 38 one day with their father's laser razor. It had been a close shave.

Rodney was indignant. "Clutz is a great robot," he said. "He can do anything any other robot can."

"Clutch?" Taurus snorted. "What kind of a name is Clutch?"

"*Clutz,*" said Rodney. "Combined Level Unit/ Type Z. He was a pioneer in the field."

"I'll bet," said Taurus.

"You'll bet what?" demanded Rodney. Taurus Johnson was such a pain.

"I'll bet my robot is better than your robot," said Taurus. "I'll even prove it."

"How?" asked Rodney.

"My robot can play moonball."

"Oh, yeah?" said Rodney. "Well, so can Clutz, rocketmouth. I'm teaching him myself."

"In that case," said Taurus, "how about a friendly little game? Angus and me and our robot against you and anybody you want and your robot."

"Sure," said Rodney. "Why not?" He could think of a few reasons why not, but he wasn't going to back down now.

"Good," said Taurus. "Tomorrow after school at the John Glenn court, Tower 4, 1500 hours."

"You're on," said Rodney. "Aurora will play goalie, just like always."

Aurora growled in agreement.

"Okay by me," said Taurus. "See you on the court, hotshot."

School that day was endless. Rodney sat in his instruction cubicle, drumming his fingers on the silicate desktop. Mrs. Wotek, the class proctor, had to keep reminding him to pay attention to his computer screen. But how could he concentrate on dry old twentieth-century history when his mind kept wandering to the moonball game?

What had he gotten himself into? Could Clutz do it? The Johnsons must have a Butler robot, from the sound of it. Clutz could go to pieces, literally, against competition like that. Why hadn't he kept his big mouth shut? He had played right into Taurus Johnson's hands.

Rodney squirmed miserably. He glanced over at Jonni and Tyler, but they were busy with a videodisk on the early colonization of Luna. Mrs. Wotek frowned at him and pointed to his computer screen. Rodney sighed and pressed the Run button for the third time.

A buzzer buzzed. It was 14:00:00 at last, time for classes to end. Rodney usually spent another hour in the EdSec library, synthesizing the day's lessons onto a single cassette to review on his home computer. But today he had other things to do. He waved to his friends and raced for the escalators.

Aurora was waiting outside for him, as she did every day. Rodney could see her through the glass walls of the escalator tube. He wasn't sure how she knew he had decided to pass up the library, but there she was, an hour earlier than usual. Rodney smiled. Aurora was the best dog on the planet, maybe in the whole galaxy. He ran across the plaza with her and hopped onto the moving walkway that carried them to and from EdSec.

The walkways ran along each side of the autojet

speedways. Of course, there weren't too many ground vehicles anymore. Most people used heli-jets. But there were lots of blue-and-silver jetbuses, which zipped along in their own special lanes on a thin cushion of air. Here and there walkways flowed over or under the speedways to allow pedestrians to get from one side to the other.

It took eight minutes at walkway speed for Rodney and Aurora to reach the John Glenn Living Complex. They rode up to Level 99 in the round, glass-walled elevator in the core of Tower 3, where they were admitted to their living unit by the automatic recognition device in the front door.

Clutz was in the leisure room, sitting on a float-a-lounge. He was holding a dustcloth tightly in both hands and staring at the telecommunicator. It was projecting a popular tridimensional holo-show called *Galactic Spy*. As Rodney came in, a major battle was taking place between a huge alien spaceship and the U.F.N.A. fleet. It was looking pretty bad for the home team.

"Clutz, we're here," he called. A missile appeared to whiz by overhead and explode near his ear. He ducked as another "grazed" his fore-

head. Laser transmission was so realistic! "Clutz?" he yelled over the din.

"Oh, Rodney, this is so exciting," answered Clutz. "Come and see. The humans are in grave danger. But they will triumph, I know they will."

The tattered remnants of the U.F.N.A. fleet made a final run. There was a deafening explosion as great chunks of alien spaceship were blasted through space and "into" the leisure room. Clutz hid his head under the dustcloth and shivered in terrified delight.

"They did it!" he squealed. "I knew they'd do it!"

Music now filled the leisure room, and an attractive young woman began demonstrating how to make sculpture for fun and profit from used insta-meal trays. Clutz sighed and touched the Off button.

"I just love *Galactic Spy*," he said. "I try never to miss it. It's so wonderful the way the humans always triumph over evil. Especially Captain Stalwart. He's my hero."

Rodney sat down on the float-a-lounge and put his arm around the robot. "How would *you* like to be a hero?" he asked.

"Oh, Rodney, me? I'm just a robot." Clutz's ear spring trembled.

"You could be a robot hero," said Rodney. "For service beyond the call of duty."

"But there are no limits to a robot's duty," said Clutz. "We serve humanity any and every way we can."

"Then if I asked you to do something you weren't specifically programmed to do," said Rodney, "could you do it anyway, for humanity— I mean, for me?" He studied the robot. "Do you think you could learn to play my favorite sport if it would help me?"

"On that basis—to help a human—my memory banks are programmed to receive new knowledge. However, my exterior form . . ." He looked embarrassed. "I know I am less than graceful."

Rodney was getting excited. "That won't matter with moonball. You'll see," he said. "Come on." He grabbed the robot by the hand, and they clattered through the front door to the elevator. Aurora ran after them.

A few minutes later they were standing in a special room in a subbasement of the John Glenn Living Complex. At least they were trying to stand. The artificial one-sixth gravity made it hard to keep from bouncing upward with every movement.

"This is a moonball court, Clutz," Rodney explained. "It has gravity just like the moon's, so players can handle the ball. Otherwise it would be too heavy."

He bent over and picked up a large white plastoid ball, one meter in diameter. In Earth gravity it weighed sixteen kilos, almost half as much as Rodney. But in Moon gravity it weighed only

about two and a half kilos. Of course, with reduced gravity Rodney's Earth-conditioned mus-
cles had no trouble lifting an object nearly half
his own weight.

He tossed the ball to Clutz. Startled, the robot
pushed it away—and found himself carried backward and up by the impact. He flailed his feet
wildly. But then, as he floated back down to the
floor, a delighted grin spread over his face.

"It's like parachute-jumping," he said. "Or
bouncing on a trampoline in slow motion. Or
free-falling through space."

"Have you done all those things?" asked Rodney
with interest.

"Heaven forbid," said Clutz.

"Well," Rodney said, "do you think you can
keep your balance and throw the ball?"

"I'll try," said Clutz.

Rodney tossed him the ball. Clutz spread his
arms wide, but the big white ball bounced off his
breastplate. The spring in his ear shuddered, and
he sailed downcourt, landing on his back, arms
and legs akimbo.

"It's not as easy as it looks," he said.

"Don't worry, everybody falls at first." Rodney

ran in slow, graceful bounds to help him up. "Try throwing to me," he said.

Clutz hopped stiffly over to the ball. With each step the spring in his ear bounced up and down like a yo-yo.

"Get ready, Rodney, here it comes," he called.

Clutz raised the ball over his head with both hands and pushed. Rodney had to jump several feet into the air, but he caught it.

"Great," he called. "Try again."

The robot gave a little leap of happiness. Rodney threw the ball back to him. This time Clutz intercepted it with one hand and managed to grab it without falling.

Rodney felt a surge of triumph. It was going to work! Clutz was going to learn moonball!

"You can do it!" he cried. "I *knew* you could."

"I can do it!" echoed Clutz happily. "I can do it!" He jumped into the air with the ball, forgetting for a moment about the lack of gravity. *Whang!* he smacked against the ceiling and landed back on the floor with a crash. The ball followed him down, bouncing off the top of his head and into Rodney's arms.

"Well, I can almost do it," he said.

Rodney helped Clutz to his feet. "You'll get it," he said. "I know you will. Here's how the game works.

"See the big metal ring fastened to the wall at the edge of the court? It's five meters up from the floor. The idea is to get the moonball away from the other team and put it through the moonring for a goal. Meanwhile they're trying to score by getting the ball into the moonring themselves. Got it so far?"

Clutz nodded.

"There are three players on each team," Rodney continued. "A fullback, a forward, and a goalie, who stays under the moonring and tries to keep the other team from scoring. Aurora is our goalie. She's really good. Show him, girl."

Aurora took up her position under the moonring. She glared at Clutz, daring him to try to score.

Rodney grasped the moonball, faked a pass to Clutz, then bounded down the court toward the moonring. When he had almost reached it, he feinted to the left and tossed the ball to the right. As Aurora dodged to meet it Rodney bounced up and pushed the ball hard toward the moonring.

But Aurora was too quick for him. Leaping high, she intercepted the ball with her shoulder and sent it sailing back toward midcourt. Clutz ducked as it floated past his head.

"Great interception, girl!" called Rodney. "Okay, Clutz. Ready to try a game?" He passed the ball gently to the robot.

Clutz wobbled toward the moonring, grasping the ball with both arms. As he neared the goal Aurora began to growl under her breath. Clutz backed away. He danced to the left, then to the right, trying to find an opening. But Aurora easily blocked each move.

Clutz grew more and more nervous. He bounced back and forth, holding tightly to the ball. He squeezed so hard that it popped out of his grasp like a banana out of its peel. Flustered, he scrambled down the court after it. Aurora yawned and lay down under the moonring.

Clutz finally got his arms around the moonball and again started for the goal. In a flash Aurora was on her feet, ears laid back, a rumble in her throat. Clutz stopped in his tracks.

"Rodney," he said, "I think my hives are starting to itch again. Do you suppose we could practice without a goalie until I really get the hang of it?"

Rodney laughed. "Sure. We'll start off easy. Aurora, go on back to the sidelines. That's a good girl."

Aurora moved slowly toward the edge of the court, muttering darkly. As she passed Clutz she suddenly leaped forward, knocking the robot off balance and sending the moonball upward with her nose, into the moonring. Clutz somersaulted toward the ceiling, the automatic scoreboard registered 1, and Aurora sauntered daintily off the court.

·5·

It was after 15:00:00 on Tuesday when they got to the moonball court. Rodney had had to do some more convincing to get Clutz to agree to play.

"You've got to do it," he argued. "You said it was your duty to keep me happy, didn't you?"

"Of course, Rodney," said Clutz. "But if we lose because of me, you'll feel less happy than if I don't play at all. Can't you tell them I had to go in for emergency repairs?"

"They wouldn't believe me," said Rodney. "They'd think I was afraid to go through with it.

Or else they'd just insist we play some other time. No, we've got to do it."

In the end Clutz agreed. What choice did he have? Sunk in gloom, he followed Rodney into the elevator.

"Well, well," said Taurus. "Here at last. We thought you'd chickened out."

"We'll show you who's chicken," said Rodney with more confidence than he felt. He looked around the court. Most of the kids in the complex were there. Word sure traveled fast.

Clutz was mumbling nervously to himself. He kept eyeing the tall, sleek, silver-and-black robot lounging at the edge of the court. The robot's red-lit eyes were sharp and penetrating, his white gloves spotless. His elegant body seemed relaxed, yet poised for action. Rodney swallowed hard.

Taurus grinned. "Allow me to make the introductions," he said. He crooked his finger and the Butler robot glided gracefully over.

"Meet Slick," he said, draping an arm over the robot's shoulder. "Best robot in the Northeast Sector."

"Delighted," said the robot in mellifluous tones that Rodney remembered well.

"This is Clutz," said Rodney, giving him a re-assuring pat on the back.

"*Argle,*" said Clutz in a strangled voice.

"Do we have a referee?" asked Rodney.

"Here." Tyler Khan bounced onto the court. He pulled a whistle out of his pocket and gave a shrill tweet.

"Okay, guys—and girls—take your positions and play moonball!"

Aurora trot-floated down to the scoring end of the court. Angus Johnson was already there, under the large metal ring. Clutz and the Butler robot moved to the middle of the court, sizing each other up, while Rodney and Taurus Johnson bounced their way to the far end and faced off on opposite sides of the moonball.

The referee blew his whistle again, and the two boys struggled for possession of the ball. They grappled back and forth, a shove by one sending the other sailing through the air. It was important to stay inside the court. Landing out of bounds gave possession of the ball to the other team.

In the first few minutes Tyler called fouls on both sides. Then Rodney got his arms around the big white ball and sent it arcing toward midcourt. Clutz and the Butler robot both leaped toward it.

"Careful, Type Z," hissed the Butler. "At your age one mustn't overdo." He gave Clutz a fierce shove that threw him off-balance and out of the court. "Foul!" yelled Rodney, but Taurus Johnson leaped forward to snatch the ball in midair and continued toward the scoring zone. Rodney turned and galloped after him.

Two meters from the ring, Taurus lobbed the ball back over Rodney's head to the Butler robot, who rushed forward and deposited it in the ring. Aurora leaped to intercept, but was pushed off-balance by Angus. Clutz picked himself up off the sidelines and straightened his breastplate. The spectators tittered. The score was 1–0.

"Ready to concede, Pentax?" asked Taurus.

"We're just getting warmed up," said Rodney.

They faced off again and moved downcourt. With the ball in midcourt the Butler robot grabbed for it.

"Out of my way, primitive mechanism," he sneered at Clutz.

"PRIMITIVE MECHANISM!" shrieked

Clutz. He jumped up and fastened both arms around the robot as the ball sailed by. Rodney caught it and shoved hard. The ball flew toward the ring. Aurora leaped toward Angus Johnson, baring her teeth and growling ferociously. Angus backed away in spite of himself, and the score was 1–1.

"Yay!" yelled the crowd.

"End first period," yelled Tyler, blowing his whistle.

Rodney huddled in one corner with his teammates. "We've done a pretty good job so far," he said. "We just have to keep the pressure on and not let them think we're running scared."

"Terrified is more like it," said Clutz. "If only Captain Stalwart were here."

"Never mind Captain Stalwart," said Rodney. "Just pay attention, and don't let that silver smoothie get to you." Clutz nodded and tried to look determined.

They bounced onto the court in a show of confidence. The crowd cheered. The Johnsons came onto the court to an equal chorus of boosters.

With the Butler's help Taurus scored two

quick goals. Then everyone gasped as a sleek black-and-silver apparition flew down from mid-court to score single-handed.

It was now 4–1.

Miraculously Rodney and Clutz managed to put together a goal between them. Then, catching Angus off-guard, Aurora deflected a Johnson field shot and nosed the ball in herself. The score was 4–3.

"Okay, Clutz," yelled Rodney. "Let's even it up."

The ball sailed down the court. Clutz grabbed it just as the Butler robot crashed into him hard from behind.

"H-E-E-L-L-P!" cried Clutz, as he and the ball flew toward the ring together.

"Let go of it!" yelled Rodney. He and Taurus headed for the scoring zone.

There was a free-for-all under the ring. Arms and legs and pink fur were everywhere. Then Clutz emerged from the heap of bodies, still grasping the ball. He leaped for the ring. The Butler robot leaped with him and pushed. The referee blew his whistle. The ball sailed back out over the players' heads, leaving Clutz draped like a rag doll

over the moonball ring. Tyler signaled the end of the game.

"Well, Pentax, I guess that proves it," said Taurus. He jumped up to the moonring and pulled Clutz free. The robot dropped to the floor with a metallic clatter.

Rodney helped Clutz to the sidelines and sat him down on a bench.

"I feel dizzy," said Clutz.

"The best team won! The best robot won!" Taurus yelled to the spectators. He raised the Butler's arm in victory. "I know a good scrap dealer, if you want to get rid of that thing" was his parting shot to Rodney. Then he and Angus and the Butler robot marched off the court.

Clutz sat on the bench with his head in his hands.

"I let you down," he moaned. "I embarrassed you in front of all your friends. I brought shame to the names of Pentax and Type Z. The only thing left for me to do is self-destruct." He clenched his fists and started to heat up his circuits. His ear spring vibrated, and his tarnished brass face turned bronze.

Rodney was alarmed. "Come on, Clutz," he said.

"You don't have to go that far. Moonball isn't everything. Besides, it was dumb of me to get suckered in by that helium-brain Taurus in the first place."

"But your honor was at stake," said Clutz, letting his circuits cool down just a notch. "And I defended it by making a fool of myself." He stared dully at the court.

Rodney grinned. "You did look pretty funny hanging up there."

"He sure did," said Tyler, swinging his whistle around his finger by its chain. "I never saw anybody get stuck on a moonball ring before. I wouldn't have missed it for anything." He bent down to pet Aurora. "You did a great job, girl. You can outplay Angus Johnson any day." Aurora gave him a large wet kiss.

"Yeah, you made 'em work for it," said Danno and Jonni. "When's the rematch?"

Clutz looked around at Rodney's friends. His face slowly regained its normal color. "You're not ashamed of me?" he asked.

Rodney put his arm around Clutz. "Anybody would rather win than lose, especially against a quark like Taurus Johnson. But you tried your

hardest, just for me. Nobody can do more than
that for a friend. I appreciate it, and I'm proud of
you."

Clutz's eyes shone. He stopped trembling and
took Rodney's hand. "The wisdom of a human,"
he said, "is boundless."

6

They moved swiftly along the Grand Central Walkway. "How much farther?" asked Clutz, trying to read the passing street signs. "I'm so excited, I can't wait!"

"We're almost there," said Rodney. He took Clutz by the arm. "Watch your step. This is where we get off."

Clutz stumbled along the exit lane with Rodney and onto the stationary walk. "Are we there yet?" he asked.

"It's just around the corner," said Rodney.

They turned the corner and were face to face with a gigantic silvery skyscraper. It filled an entire double block. Clutz looked up and gasped. There were no windows in the gleaming tower, no openings of any kind except a pair of huge metal doors. The door on the left was engraved with the letters *F. O.* The right one said *R. K.*

"What a big building," said Clutz.

"The biggest in the whole Northeast Sector," said Rodney. "It's 301 levels. It's so cold on the top level that they pump air from up there and use it to cool the rest of the building. In winter—"

"Welcome to the global headquarters of Food on Request Korp," said a liquid, feminine voice from somewhere above them. *"We are not open to the public. Have you the proper authorization to enter?"*

Rodney reached into his jumpsuit pocket and pulled out a white plastoid card. Across the top of it was printed LYRA PENTAX, 074A136-S, and underneath, SON RODNEY. At the bottom were small color pictures of each of them. Rodney inserted the card in a slot to the left of the door and pulled it again.

"Thank you," said the lovely voice. *"You may*

enter." The doors slid open with a whoosh. *F.O.* disappeared into the left wall and *R.K.* into the right.

"Come on," said Rodney, grabbing Clutz's hand.

They entered the huge metal-walled lobby. "Are you sure you know the way to your mother's office?" Clutz whispered. "What if we get lost in here and never find our way out?"

"Of course I know the way, silly," said Rodney. "I've been here lots of times. All we do is follow the signs. See?" He pointed. "Just like a trail."

Clutz looked up. In each of the corridors leading off the lobby like the arms of an octopus, rows of small plastoid signs were mounted on the walls. One row was now flashing * THIS WAY PLEASE * in mauve letters.

"They're programmed by my I.D. card to show us the way to Mom's office," said Rodney. Clutz hurried after him as he ran down the hall.

The trail of light ended at an elevator bank deep in the heart of F.O.R.K. They stepped into one of the cylindrical elevators.

"What level?" asked Clutz, studying the glowing elevator walls. "I want to press the button."

"There aren't any buttons in F.O.R.K.'s ele-vators," said Rodney. "Security reasons. They automatically take you to the right level."

"Ooooooooh," said Clutz as they rose in a single swift motion. They stopped smoothly at Level 178, and the door slid open. More corridors led away from the elevator.

"This way," said Rodney, following another series of flashing lights.

At the end the long corridor opened into a vast area filled with all sorts of activity. A steady hum emanated from a computer bank in one corner. The remainder of the room was filled with hundreds of typewriterlike terminals, blinking and chattering like mechanical monkeys. People rushed back and forth around them with arm-fuls of order forms, magnetic bubble cartridges, and printout tapes.

"Mom's office is in there," said Rodney, point-ing to a row of glass-walled cubicles.

Lyra Pentax was a subregional coordinating supervisor of the F.O.R.K. Distribution Center. The Center was U.F.N.A. headquarters for the mammoth Food on Request Korp., whose offices spanned the globe. In the old days, Rodney knew, people had gone to places called supermarkets to buy their food each week. What a pain that must have been. Today all you had to do was touch a few buttons on the F.O.R.K.–installed "Cook's Helper" found in every modern kitchen. A few minutes later everything arrived by vacuum chute and was deposited right in the cryobin. Millions of people depended on F.O.R.K. every day. It made Rodney proud to think that his mother helped keep the whole system working smoothly and efficiently.

He and Clutz zigzagged through the confusion.

"Rodney!" called Mrs. Pentax. "Over here!"

Lyra Pentax was seated at a computer terminal in the center of the room. A writing stylus was stuck behind one ear, and she was leafing through a heap of order forms on the desk next to the terminal.

"Hi, Mom," said Rodney. "You don't mind my bringing Clutz, do you? He really wanted to come."

Mrs. Pentax ran her fingers through her hair. "This really isn't a very good day for it," she said.

"I'm terribly busy. We were told this morning that we had to program in the basic orders of all new F.O.R.K. customers before the end of the day. No one knows why. We usually have a week from the time a customer signs up to the date of the first delivery. I'm checking now to see how things are coming along."

Mrs. Pentax punched in a few commands, the terminal chattered briefly, and rows of letters and numbers appeared on the small videoscreen above it.

"Can I print something?" asked Rodney. "I want to show Clutz how my name comes up on the screen when I put in my number."

"Maybe later," said Mrs. Pentax. "The programmer assigned to this terminal has to get back to work now. But I'll give you a quick tour of Northeast Sector operations. That's about all the time I can spare today."

"That would be most edifying," said Clutz.

"Great," said Rodney. "I've never had a real tour of the place before."

Mrs. Pentax led them to the far end of the room. A section of the wall was encased in metal and covered with knobs and dials. It hummed softly.

Attendants in white tunics kept checking the dials and putting in and taking out small crystalline bubble cartridges in which millions of bits of information were stored.

"This is the main computer for our department," said Mrs. Pentax.

"It looks like the one where I found your address," said Clutz.

"It is probably similar," said Mrs. Pentax. "But it contains much more than just the names and addresses of F.O.R.K.'s customers. It also has stored inside it on hundreds of tiny chips the basic order for every household we supply—that is, the foods and other items that a family wishes to receive each week automatically."

"Like my chocofreez," said Rodney.

"That's right," said his mother. "Customers can also request new things or change their orders. That's all recorded by the computer as well, so they can be charged for it."

"Where is the food?" asked Clutz.

"It's stored in cryobin compartments on our middle levels," said Mrs. Pentax. "When the computer up here sends electronic commands to the autodelivery system on the bottom levels, the items are automatically dropped into the right pneumatic chutes and sent to the households that want them."

"Sort of like a brain, a stomach, and feet," said Rodney. "Neat."

"Neat," echoed Clutz. "But what are all those little video typewriters for?"

"Terminals," said Mrs. Pentax. "They're much more than just typewriters. They are what we use to 'talk' with the computer. We give commands and questions in a language it understands, and it prints back its answers."

They stopped in front of a terminal that was clacking away ferociously.

"What is it doing?" asked Clutz.

"It's asking about basic orders of old customers," said Mrs. Pentax.

Clutz was transfixed. "It is speaking, in its way, as I speak in mine. It is communicating. Although it is a machine, it is a thinking being. Cousin!" He threw his arms around the terminal and embraced it. The machine clattered briefly, then doubled its frenzy.

Mrs. Pentax leaped forward. "Clutz, what did you do?"

"Do?" asked Clutz.

"I think he pressed something," said Rodney.

"A *2*. He hit the number *2*," said Mrs. Pentax, peering at the videoscreen. "This is awful."

"What's so awful about pressing one little number?" asked Rodney. "He didn't mean to."

"That's not the point," said his mother. "The computer was asking if it should activate delivery of old basic orders as well as new ones. Clutz answered *2*, which to our computer means *double* the normal order! Clutz has just delivered a two-week supply of all food and nonfood items to every customer in the Northeast Sector. They'll all be furious, and so will my boss!"

"Then cancel the order," said Rodney. "Just tell the computer to forget the whole thing."

"I can't," said Mrs. Pentax. "Computers function instantaneously, in picoseconds. That's a trillionth of a second! The order was carried out as soon as Clutz pushed the key."

"They couldn't have dumped all that stuff in everybody's cryobin in one picosecond," said Rodney.

"No," said Mrs. Pentax, "but the order goes to

the cryocomputer downstairs that fast, and it's automatic from that point on. It takes a complete override to correct the error, which would shut down the whole system. Do you know what it means to shut down this whole system? We only do it in real emergencies." She began pacing back and forth.

"PENTAX!" A large screen near the ceiling lit up, and the face of a heavyset woman with blue hair exploded onto it.

"Yes, Miss O'Dwork," answered Lyra Pentax.

"Pentax! It's an emergency! Our customers are not going to stand for it. And they're certainly not going to go hungry!"

"Hungry?"

"When their food supply runs out. We've been expecting it, but we'd hoped it could be avoided. There's been a power breakdown in the N-1 computer monitoring the Northeast Sector—your sector. It won't be fully operational for several days. Something about an overload disrupting the electron flow patterns in the power core. Some households will be without a F.O.R.K. delivery for two full weeks! We have to find a way out of this, even if it means air-dropping groceries from helijets!''

"Miss O'Dwork, I believe I know what caused the overload," said Rodney's mother.

"You do? Good work, Pentax. Let's hear it. Maybe we can prevent its happening again.''

"Could a doubling of all basic orders cause the computer to overload?''

"It might," said Miss O'Dwork.

"But what about all those new customers you've been cramming into it all day?'' Rodney put in. "I'll bet that many new orders could overload things, too, all at once.''

"True, young man," said Miss O'Dwork. "The straw that broke the urdro's back, as they say. But that still leaves us with the problem of hungry people and no way to feed them.''

"Miss O'Dwork, I think somebody solved the problem," said Rodney.

"How?" asked Miss O'Dwork.

"That's what I've been trying to tell you, Miss O'D.," said Mrs. Pentax. "The computer was just instructed to double every basic order in the entire sector. It was an acci—''

"Pentax! Is that true? Do you know what it means?" demanded Miss O'Dwork. "Believe me, the board of directors will hear about this. How did you anticipate so closely?"

"But I didn't—"

"Mom accepts full responsibility," said Rodney.

"And so she should," said Miss O'Dwork. "Carry on, Pentax. And while you're about it, get that robot's ear fixed." The videoscreen went dark.

"Clutz!" said Lyra Pentax. "I'd almost forgotten you were here. Come out from behind that terminal."

Clutz peeked around the corner. "Is she gone?" he asked. The spring in his ear was bobbing violently. "Are you in terrible trouble? Am I?"

"I don't know yet," said Mrs. Pentax. "The board will undoubtedly want to know more about this incident. I could be accused of negligence." She frowned. "You two had better leave now, before anything else happens."

"Oh, yes, madam, by all means," said Clutz. "It has been an unforgettable experience. But I must get home as quickly as possible in any case."

"Why?" asked Rodney.

Clutz looked sheepish. "Because," he said, "I must find room in the kitchen for a two-week, double-size delivery from F.O.R.K." He fluttered a little wave at Mrs. Pentax and tottered toward the elevators.

"Excellent dinner, Clutz," said Mr. Pentax, easing himself into a float-a-lounge. "You're becoming quite a cook."

"Thank you, sir," said Clutz. "I wanted to make up in some way for the difficulties I caused Madam at F.O.R.K. this afternoon."

"Difficulties? Oh, blast!" said Arthur Pentax, fiddling with the touch sensors on the console next to his chair.

Mrs. Pentax looked up from the book-film she was viewing. "What is it, dear?"

"Something's wrong with the telecom," said Mr. Pentax, glaring at the wall screen. "Just when I wanted to see *Nightly Newsminutes*."

Rodney was lying on the floor with his pocket recorder. Clutz had been helping him prepare a report for technology class on the history of combined-level robots.

"Wow! Look at that," he said, sitting up. "*'.enecs strops citcalagretni eht no tsetal eht won dnA'* It's running everything backward! Switch to holovision, Dad. This oughta be good."

Mr. Pentax touched a button on the console. Suddenly a man and a woman materialized on the screen and backed away from each other with arms outstretched. The man backed out through a door that opened behind him. The door closed. "*,ni emoC*" said the woman, sitting down. There was a knock on the door.

Mr. Pentax turned off the holovision in disgust.

"Hey, Dad, leave it on—it was getting interesting," said Rodney.

"Not now, Son," said Mr. Pentax. "I want to call the repair service and see how quickly we can get the thing fixed." He pressed the videophone number scanner. Rows of names and numbers skimmed across the small screen.

"Here we are: 'Stellar Telekorp., Service Department. Evenings and holidays, phone 212-7598-6002S.'" He punched the number into the videophone.

"Thank you for calling Stellar Telekorp., communicators to the world," said an attractive young lady with platinum hair and lavender eyes. "I am a visual recording. Our service department is closed for the day. However, we are now accepting appointments for Monday, the twenty-fifth. When you see the red light, kindly leave your name and number, and a communications technician will return your call." A red light shone above the girl's gleaming head. Mr. Pentax left his name and number and hung up.

"Monday, the twenty-fifth," he said. "That's more than a week away. What am I supposed to do for *Nightly Newsminutes* in the meantime?"

"It can't be helped, dear," said Mrs. Pentax.

"Unless—" said Clutz.

"Unless what?" asked Rodney.

"Oh, nothing, Rodney," said Clutz. "Shall we get back to work on your report?"

The next afternoon, when Rodney came home from school, he was shocked nearly speechless. There was Clutz on his knees in front of the telecommunicator console. He had taken the top off the machine, and both hands were plunged deep into its bowels. Scattered all around him on the floor were hundreds of tiny magnetic crystal bubbles of different shapes and colors.

"Clutz," Rodney gasped. "What are you *doing*?"

Clutz looked up with a surprised smile. "Why, Rodney, is it time for you to come home already? I've been so absorbed in my work that I lost track of the time."

"Your *work*?" Rodney struggled to stay calm. "Clutz, what have you done to the telecom?"

"Why, Rodney, can't you see? I'm fixing it. I just couldn't bear the thought of watching Captain Stalwart do everything backward. It would be so terribly—undignified. And your father enjoys his *Nightly Newsminutes* so much. This will mean a great deal to him."

"But what makes you think you can fix it?" asked Rodney. "You're not a communications technician."

"No, I am something much better for the purpose," said Clutz. "I am a machine. Who knows more about one machine than another machine?"

"But you're taking an awful chance," said Rodney. "If something goes wrong, my parents will really be upset. Consoles are expensive, you know."

"But I must prove myself to your mother and father," said Clutz, "and the week is nearly up. Now, would you please hand me that little pile of crystals over there? The green ones, not the blue ones."

Rodney handed Clutz the parts and sat down nervously to watch. Clutz peered inside the console, whispering and nodding and rearranging first one small crystalline piece and then another. Finally he sat back on his heels.

"That should do it," he said. He scooped up a dozen or so remaining parts and dumped them into the console. Then he snapped the top back on, stood up, and dusted off his hands.

"It's really simple when you know how," he said.

"I'll believe that when I see the results," said Rodney.

Dinner was over, and Rodney was helping Clutz take the dishes from the table to the disposal chute. Mr. and Mrs. Pentax went into the leisure room. Mr. Pentax stretched out on his favorite float-a-lounge, next to the console, and turned on the telecommunicator.

"Oh, darn, I forgot," he said. "It's broken." He started to turn it off.

"Wait, Dad," said Rodney. "Maybe the trouble was only temporary."

"*. . . price of iridium reached the thousand-credit mark today. Not since a century ago has . . .*"

"What do you know!" said Mr. Pentax. "It's working. Must have just been cosmic interference last night."

"No, it was broken, all right," said Rodney with a smile. "Clutz fixed it this afternoon. Isn't that great? Try the holovision."

"Clutz fixed it? By himself?" Mr. Pentax pressed the touch sensor. Suddenly his float-a-lounge started vibrating so hard that he almost fell out of it. He sat up and pressed the button again.

"What the—?" he yelped as the float-a-lounge took off around the room. He grabbed the chair arms. "What's going on?"

The float-a-lounge picked up speed. *"Shut it off!"* Mr. Pentax yelled frantically, ducking the ceiling and dodging the drapes.

Rodney dropped the dinner plates and ran to the console. He punched every button, but it didn't do any good. He pulled the top off and stared helplessly inside. No use—it might make things worse. He and Clutz tried to intercept the float-a-lounge as it careened wildly around the room, but they couldn't catch it. Aurora began barking and joined the chase. Mr. Pentax held on for dear life.

Mrs. Pentax jumped up from her float-a-lounge with alarm. "Arthur, you come down from there!" she demanded.

"Duck!" yelled Rodney as the lounge turned and bore down on them all.

The float-a-lounge zoomed out of the leisure room toward the front door. "Oh, no," cried Arthur Pentax. "Somebody *do* something!"

The sensor-activated door slid open, and Mr. Pentax flew out into the hallway core of Level 99. Doors around the circular hall slid open as neighbors peered out to see what all the commotion was about.

"Look out!" yelled Rodney's father, nearly de-capitating Mrs. Fenster from 99C. The old lady dived for the floor.

Jason Kreel, the Pentaxes' next-door neighbor, opened his door and stepped into the hall. "Hey, Arthur," he said, "you'd better stop fooling around before someone gets hurt."

"I wish I could," wailed Mr. Pentax, sailing past him into the Kreels' living unit.

A gigantic metal mobile hung from the Kreels' leisure room ceiling. The float-a-lounge tunneled through the middle of it with a tremendous clatter. Wires and bits of metal flew everywhere. Mr. Pentax was battered and desperate. How could he stop his space-age flying carpet? He grabbed hold of a tall potted plant as he flew past. The whole plant came out of its pot in his hands.

"MY RARE VENUSIAN FLYTRAP!" shrieked Mrs. Kreel. She ran after Rodney's fa-ther, trying to grab the plant by its roots. Nutri-ent solution and broken Venusian flytrap leaves rained down around her onto the floor.

Arthur Pentax glanced ahead, groaned, and dropped the plant as the float-a-lounge headed for the Kreels' balcony. The large sliding glass doors were open. Gauzy curtains fluttered in the early evening breeze. Grabbing the curtains in a last effort to stop himself, Rodney's father sailed through the opening, into the sunset. The curtains came off in his hands and wrapped themselves around his neck like the scarf of a World War I fighter pilot.

Mrs. Pentax, Rodney, Clutz, and Aurora ran into the Kreels' living unit and out onto the balcony in time to see him head off toward the horizon, the curtains streaming out behind him.

"Come back," squeaked Clutz.

"Come on," said Mrs. Pentax. "We've got to follow that lounge." They ran out of the living unit and into the elevator.

By the time they got outside, the sky was alive with activity. Helijets were zigzagging crazily. Sirens screamed and police searchlights crisscrossed above the glass-domed rooftops.

"Arthur!" cried Lyra Pentax.

"There he is!" yelled Rodney, pointing to a small object whizzing in and out of traffic, 300 meters up.

A police helijet gave chase. As the helijet closed in, a cable with a hook on the end snaked out to

snag the bottom of the float-a-lounge. But each time the hook reached out, the float-a-lounge shifted direction. Mr. Pentax was carried back and forth like a leaf in the wind.

Trembling, Rodney's father wrapped both legs around his perilous perch. He leaned over and tried to grab the cable with his hands. For one shuddering moment he almost had it. Then he lost his balance.

Rodney's heart leaped into his throat. "Hold on, Dad!" he shrieked. He closed his eyes, afraid to look up.

Above Rodney's head Arthur Pentax whimpered softly, closed his eyes, and held on, afraid to look down.

The helijet made another pass. This time the hook caught and set firmly. Like a fish on a line, Mr. Pentax and the float-a-lounge were pulled to the ground. Rodney's father was safe.

Attached to the cable, the float-a-lounge still bucked and swung around like a wild thing. Mr. Pentax took a deep breath and rolled off, into a bed of red chrysanthemoons. He lay sprawled there in a daze. One of the skycops drew his laser gun and fired at the writhing float-a-lounge. It shuddered, twitched, and lay still at last.

A crowd gathered around Mr. Pentax. Rodney, his mother, Clutz, and Aurora pushed their way through to him.

"Arthur, are you all right?" asked Mrs. Pentax, throwing her arms around him. She and Rodney helped him to his feet.

"I made it," Arthur Pentax said shakily.

"Yes, dear, thank goodness," said Mrs. Pentax. "It was awful. The float-a-lounge just went berserk."

"Perhaps," volunteered Clutz, "when I repaired the console— Some further adjustment must be necessary."

Rodney tried to signal Clutz to be quiet. But the robot was too absorbed in his own thoughts.

"Maybe," he said, "if I switch the F83 blue crystals and the green C28's, that would refocus the directive impulse. Yes, I do believe that could be it. Mr. Pentax, sir, I think I know the cause of the problem."

Arthur Pentax came out of his daze. He fixed his bloodshot eyes on the robot. "Never mind," he said grimly. "I already know the cause of the problem."

"Well, now, isn't that wonderful," said a skycop, coming over with his ticket book in his hand. "I'm sure the judge will be fascinated when you tell him."

"Judge?" said Rodney.

"That's right, son," said the skycop. "Your father here is going to have a nice long talk with the Subsector 3 aerial traffic judge." Mr. Pentax numbly put out his hand and the skycop dropped half a dozen summonses into it.

"But, Officer, it was all an accident. He didn't mean to do anything wrong," said Rodney.

"The judge will be so glad to know that," said the skycop. He removed the cable from the float-a-lounge, got into his helijet, and lifted off.

The crowd parted to let them through as the Pentaxes started back toward their living unit. Mr. Pentax, still wobbly on his feet, clutched his fistful of summonses with one hand and his wife's arm with the other. The Kreels' white curtains were still wrapped around his neck. Clutz thoughtfully picked up the ends and carried them so they wouldn't get dirty.

Rodney glanced back at the smoking float-a-lounge. Two little boys were bouncing on it and pretending to steer it through the sky. Rodney took his father's free arm.

"I could have been killed," Arthur Pentax said to his son. "Do you realize that? And it was all that cock eyed robot's fault."

Behind them, unaware of the conversation, Clutz was busily trying to figure out where his calculations had gone wrong.

Rodney started to speak. "No," said Mr. Pentax, stopping him, "I don't want to hear any explanations or excuses. Tomorrow he goes."

·8·

Tomorrow he goes. Tomorrow he goes. The words spun around relentlessly inside Rodney's head. It was what he had feared since Clutz had arrived, what he had tried not to think about.

All the way home Rodney was unable to speak. He didn't want to say anything for fear Clutz would know the truth. Rodney didn't want him to know—not yet, anyway. Maybe he could persuade his father to change his mind. There was always that chance, even if it was a slim one.

They stepped off the elevator and walked toward

the door of their living unit. As they crossed the hall Mrs. Kreel dashed out of her doorway and snatched the curtains from around Arthur Pentax's neck.

"You can expect a substantial bill for damages," she snapped. Mr. Pentax nodded mutely. Mrs. Kreel turned and marched back inside.

The Pentaxes went into their own living unit. The door slid shut behind them automatically.

"I'm exhausted," said Arthur Pentax, rubbing his eyes. "I'm going to bed."

"But, Dad," Rodney begged, "I've got to talk to you."

"I'm much too tired now, Rodney. Besides, there's nothing to discuss. My mind is made up."

"Please, Dad," Rodney pleaded. "This affects me as much as you and Mom. You've got to hear my side of it. You've just got to."

Mr. Pentax sighed. "All right, Son. We'll talk while I put on my sleepsuit. But I told you, my mind is made up."

Rodney and his parents went into the bedroom and closed the door. Aurora scratched on the closed door, which slid open to admit her, then closed again.

Clutz, left alone in the leisure room, looked around for something to do. He wandered over to the visual center and scanned the rack of holovision discs. He chose his favorite, "Captain Stalwart Fights the Gworkon Menace," and inserted it into the console. He started to sit down on a float-a-lounge, then thought better of it and stretched out on the floor.

He could hear the Pentaxes arguing about something in the bedroom. ". . . didn't do it on purpose," Rodney was saying. ". . . won't let it happen again." Clutz felt it was wrong to eavesdrop on private family matters. He directed his attention to the holoshow.

A familiar heroic figure materialized on the wallscreen and began pacing back and forth. Captain Stalwart was really in a jam this time. The evil Gworks from the planet Gworkon had kidnapped his beloved, the beautiful Concertina. Unless he surrendered himself—and the plans to the new top-secret U238XL—before dawn, the lovely Concertina would be vaporized to smithereens.

But when *was* dawn on a planet that circled two suns? Captain Stalwart had to think fast.

". . . and I want him out of here—fast!" Arthur Pentax was saying. As Clutz watched Captain Stalwart wrestle with the fine points of Gworkon astronomy, another verbal wrestling match was taking place on his behalf.

"It's just not fair," Rodney argued. "You promised he could stay a week and it hasn't been a week yet. You've got to give him more time!"

Captain Stalwart was in a race against time. A set of fake plans in a cylinder by his side, he rocketed toward Gworkon and destiny. It was growing lighter by the microsecond.

Suddenly dawn broke. Clutz sat bolt upright on the floor as the truth flooded his circuits. The voices in the bedroom—they were arguing about *him*! They wanted him to go!

A giant wave of desolation washed over him. They didn't want him. He had failed again, there could be no doubt about it. He had done his best, but apparently his best hadn't been good enough.

The Flotons had been right after all. His days of serving humans were over. All he was good for now was scrap. Well, if that was true, there was only one thing left for him to do—something he had almost done five days earlier. He stood up, squared his shoulders, and walked slowly into the kitchen. He stood for a moment in front of the trash-conveyor chute and then slid open the round metal door. A rush of air pulled at him, beckoning him into its black mouth. Obediently he placed one leg, and then the other, into the opening.

"Ooooooooooo-o-o-h-h," he gasped as he was sucked into the chute. The door clanged shut behind him and he was thrust blindly downward with ever-increasing speed. Objects hurled past him, rained down on him, smashed under him.

He tried to control himself, but his circuits were in chaos.

"Rodney," he called plaintively. "Mr. and Mrs. Pentax, Captain Stalwart—" No one answered.

The door of the Pentaxes' bedroom slid open and a tearful Rodney emerged.

"Just go out there and tell him," his father was saying. "You wanted to be the one to do it, and there's no point in putting it off. Tell him we'll try to find him another job. Tell him you'll come visit him. But tell him he can't stay here any longer. We said it would be on a trial basis, and the trial just ended—for all of us."

Rodney choked back a sob and trudged toward the leisure room. Aurora trotted alongside him, nuzzling his hand.

The telecom was blasting away as Captain Stalwart battled the Gworkons, but the leisure room was empty. Rodney turned off the holo-vision.

"Clutz?" he called. "Where are you?" He looked in the kitchen and in the dining room. He ran down the hall to his own room.

"Clutz? Stop fooling around. Come on out."

Aurora was sniffing around the leisure room. A low growl formed in her throat. Something was wrong. Clutz wasn't in the living unit, she could tell. Where had he gone? Had someone taken him? What if that someone came back for *her*? As Rodney came down the hall she zipped past him to the control panel and pressed the alarm button.

"There's nothing the police can do," said Mr. Pentax, turning off the alarm. "Clutz didn't really belong to us, you know. If he decided to go somewhere else, that's not a crime."

"Maybe it's for the best, dear," said Rodney's mother. "He was leaving anyway. I'm sure he'll find a new family who will take good care of him."

Rodney was less confident. He was sure now that Clutz had heard his father's ultimatum and had left in despair. He was probably far away by this time. Who knew where he might have gone or what he might have done in his state of mind?

Rodney blinked back the tears. If he could just see Clutz again and explain things. He wanted him back more than anything. He felt as if he had lost a member of his family.

Aurora whined and licked Rodney's wet cheek.

To tell the truth, she felt somewhat guilty about what had happened. She should have been more vigilant. But she had been so interested in the discussion in the bedroom that she hadn't paid attention to anything else. She was too absorbed in the thought that she would soon be free of her one rival for Rodney's affections.

Still, when she saw how totally miserable Rodney was over Clutz's disappearance, she wished the robot were back. She would endure almost anything to keep Rodney happy, even sharing him.

"Your mother is right, Son," said Mr. Pentax. "Clutz will find another family."

"But what if they feel the way you do, and he ends up as spare parts, or scrap?" Rodney sobbed. "You said we would find a good home for him, and that I could visit him. Now he might be dismantled, or even melted down. I'll never see him again, ever, and it's all your fault!" Mrs. Pentax put her arms around her son, but he broke away from her and ran out of the room.

At the bottom of the trash-conveyor chute, Clutz had been dumped unceremoniously onto a moving belt heaped with junk. He was carried from there to a central underground collection point, where a row of giant headless robots with shovels instead of hands scooped him into a huge open container. When it was full, the container moved into a tunnel leading to the main WasteSec plant. There its contents would be sorted out, melted down, and recycled for further use.

As Rodney lay in his darkened bedroom high up in the John Glenn Living Complex, Clutz was moving through a black underground tunnel, dazed, his circuits barely functioning, buried up to his neck in discarded objects.

A fitting end, Clutz thought dimly, and sighed.

Rodney tossed and turned in the darkness. He listened to Aurora snore and whimper at his feet as she dreamed of robots. Rodney thought of Clutz, alone and unhappy somewhere, and silent tears rolled down his cheeks.

On Friday Rodney's parents kept him home from school. He was pale and feverish and had no appetite. He hovered over the videophone. Every time it buzzed, he grabbed it, hoping it was news of Clutz. Each time he was disappointed. By evening his parents were really worried about him.

At dinner they all picked at their food. The fact was, the meal wasn't very good. Clutz had turned out to be a much better cook than any of them and had taken over all the food preparation. Now it was back to insta-meals.

No one felt much like cleaning up afterward, either. They sat at the table in silence.

"I stopped at Ralph's Robots today," Mrs. Pentax said finally.

"Mother!" Rodney cried. "How could you?"

"I'm sorry, Rodney, but we need help, and a robot still seems to be the answer. Nothing is decided yet. The salesman was very nice, though. He's giving us a free home trial of a Butler, starting tomorrow morning. You might like him very much, once you get to know him. Butler robots are very advanced. You can play moonball with him in the afternoon if you like."

"I *hate* Butler robots, and I'm never playing moonball again!" shouted Rodney, jumping up from the table and running out of the room.

The next morning Rodney's sleep was interrupted by a smooth, deep voice coming from the other end of the living unit. Reluctantly he opened his eyes. A clean jumpsuit and freshly polished boots were laid out at the foot of his bed, in the spot usually occupied by Aurora. He got up without enthusiasm. Ignoring the clothes, he shuffled into the leisure room.

"Master Rodney, I presume," hummed the

Butler robot. His red eyes gleamed. "Why aren't you dressed? Did the choice of clothing displease you?"

"I hate getting dressed on Saturday morning," said Rodney irritably. "Where's Aurora? Why wasn't she in my room?"

"A dog in one's bed is unsanitary," admonished the Butler. "Dogs are unsanitary. They endanger humans with their germs."

"Aurora always sleeps with me, and I've never caught anything," said Rodney.

"It is just a matter of time," said the robot. "I hate to expose my humans to unnecessary dangers."

"I'm not worried," growled Rodney. "And I'm not your human." He went into the kitchen.

"Good morning, dear," said Mrs. Pentax anxiously. "Did you sleep all right? What would you like for breakfast? Butler has prepared a whole-grain barley gruel—a Martian recipe, I believe. Very nourishing."

"Yecch," said Rodney.

"I have to agree," said his father, pushing aside his bowl. "Butler, some stimu-tea, please."

"I'm sorry, sir," said the Butler. "Stimu-tea is very harmful to the human central nervous system.

It is my duty to protect your health. May I offer you a glass of soymilk? Or vitalized citro juice, perhaps?"

"All right," grumbled Mr. Pentax. "Citro juice."

"Clutz always made us anything we wanted to eat," said Rodney. He took a breakfast bar from the cupboard and slammed the door. "I don't want anything else. I'm going to take Aurora for a walk." He stalked out of the kitchen.

"Wear a jacket—and gloves and a hat," cautioned the robot. "It's a chilly morning for humans."

Aurora stood in the elevator and nosed against Rodney's clenched fist.

"I'm sorry, girl," said Rodney. "It's not you I'm mad at." He pressed the button for Main Level. "It's that Butler robot. How can Mom and Dad think he could ever take the place of Clutz? He *never* will, even if he's the best moonball player in the whole solar system. I hate him!"

Aurora barked in agreement.

"I'm sorry he kicked you out of my bed this morning. Clutz would never have done that."

Aurora gave Rodney's hand a forgiving lick.

The elevator door opened and Aurora bounded out. Rodney hurried to catch up with her, bumping into two postal robots loaded with the day's mail for Tower 4. A bag clattered to the floor, and letter-tapes and newsfilm cylinders rolled out. Each was addressed with rows of tiny magnetic dots. Every mailbox in the lobby walls had its own unique rows of corresponding dots. The postal robots' job was to scan the walls with each piece of mail until they found the box whose address it matched, then insert it in the proper opening. They never made a mistake.

Rodney picked up the tape cylinders and hooked the mailbag to the front of one of the robots. Then he ran outside after Aurora. Shivering, he blinked at the sun glinting off the bronze glass towers of the complex. It was still early, but the walks were already filling with people, and several shops and restaurants on the main levels were open.

Rodney said hello to Mr. Fung, who was air-hosing the sidewalk in front of his Lunar-American Restaurant. Sometimes Rodney and Aurora stopped there after school, and Mrs. Fung gave them each a steamed lunabun. Rodney wondered what the Fungs served for breakfast. Not barley gruel, he was certain of that.

He followed Aurora to Tower 4, where she pushed open the door of the Special Cuts Proto Shop. Aurora always went to Special Cuts for her best bones. The butcher, Mr. Banda, was cutting up a huge side of cryodried meat with a laser saw.

"I told Aurora she could have the scraps from this Martian moss moose if she came in this afternoon," he said to Rodney. "Come back later—or send Clutz. I get such a kick out of that fellow."

Rodney choked and ran out of the shop. "What did I say?" Mr. Banda asked Aurora as he tossed her a tidbit. She caught it in her mouth and trotted after Rodney.

The two walked slowly toward the park, looking in various shop windows along the way. Rodney's heart wasn't really in it, but he stopped at his favorite, ComputoCraft, a store that sold kits for building computerized models. Rodney wondered if they had any for making full-size robots. He thought he saw something in the window that resembled Clutz, but it was only a display of bronze alloy tubing.

He and Aurora crossed over the Park South Walkway and continued past a tall green glass living complex surrounded by broad plazas. They entered the gates of ParkSec and wandered up and down the neatly geometric pathways, surrounded on either side by lush flowers. In roller lanes boys and girls and little old ladies zoomed by on jet boards or pneumo-skates. Young couples strolled, hand in hand. Robots walked dogs or pushed baby carriages or watched small children playing. There were Butlers and Nannies and several models that Rodney couldn't identify. He studied them all carefully, hopefully. But nowhere was there a Combined Level Unit/Type Z with a spring poking out of one shell-like ear.

"It's no use," he said at last, sinking onto a molded plastoid bench near a reflecting pool. Aurora flopped down at his feet and sniffed delicately at a large pink flower. She was fond of flowers, especially pink ones. She gazed at Rodney with sympathy.

"I can't get Clutz out of my mind," he said. "I keep wondering if he's still all right and if I'll ever see him again." He sighed mournfully.

They stared into the reflecting pool. Rodney

threw a small pebble into the water and watched the ripples break up their images. He threw another pebble and another.

A glint of burnished metal shone briefly on the water. Rodney looked around, but it was only the sunlight or a bit of refuse on the bottom of the pool.

Rodney stood up abruptly. "Come on," he said to Aurora. "I can't sit here anymore. Let's go home—maybe he's come back."

They left the park. When they neared the John Glenn Living Complex, Aurora barked and started off in the direction of Tower 4.

"All right, girl," said Rodney. "You go see Mr. Banda about those scraps. I'll meet you at home."

Aurora trotted off and Rodney headed for Tower 3, kicking a rock ahead of him as he walked. Clutz had to be somewhere, and Rodney realized now that, no matter what, he had to find him.

When Rodney arrived at Tower 3, Aurora was waiting in front of the elevator, a neatly wrapped package between her teeth.

"Aurora," said Rodney, "I've made a decision. We're going to find Clutz. We've got to and that's all there is to it. You don't want to be stuck with that Butler monster forever, do you?"

Aurora bared her teeth around her package and growled.

"That's what I thought," said Rodney. The elevator came and they got in.

The Butler robot was waiting for them at the door of the living unit. "Where have you been?" he demanded. "You are late for your lunch. And you went out without your jacket after all, Master Rodney. I must insist that you take better care of yourself, or I will have to do it for you."

Rodney brushed past him and went to the table. On it were a glass of soymilk and a dish containing four tablets.

"What's that?" he asked.

"That is your lunch," answered the Butler. "According to my biochemical analysis, once a day you must have two hyper-vitamins, a mineral complex, and protein concentrate. A growing boy-human needs special nourishment."

Rodney looked at him with disgust. Motioning to Aurora, he ran down the hall to his room and closed the door.

"Girl," he whispered, "here's what we'll do."

·10·

"Shhh." Rodney motioned for Aurora to be quiet. He placed the note on his pillow. Then, softly, he turned off the light and opened his bedroom door. It was nearly dark in the living unit. Mr. and Mrs. Pentax had gone out for the evening, and Rodney had told the Butler he was going to bed early.

Instead, he and Aurora now tiptoed purposefully down the dim hallway. Each carried a small travel bag. Aurora's contained her pink hairbrush, an extra ribbon, her favorite plasti-chew toy, and four Hi-Proto Doggy Dinners. Rodney had packed a clean jumpsuit, his sleepsuit, his ultrasonic self-pasting toothbrush, and some Nutri-Sweets bars. He went to the hall closet, took out his jacket, and stuffed it into the bag. Then he pulled a small plastoid rectangle out of his pocket and examined it. It was his junior credit I.D., which was issued to every U.F.N.A. child from six to twelve annums old. His had a fifty-credit spending limit, raised from forty on his last birthday. That wasn't much, but it would pay for a couple of days food and shelter if necessary. Rodney added it to his bag.

In the unlit kitchen the Butler robot was working briskly, using his infrared vision, to prepare some healthful concoction for Sunday breakfast. At the same time he had decided that the whole kitchen needed a thorough cleaning and had pulled out the contents of every drawer and cupboard. Food packages and kitchen utensils were heaped everywhere. Rodney and Aurora waited until the robot's head was hidden behind a stack of disposa-plates. Then they slid open the front door of the living unit and hurried out.

Luckily no one was in the elevator. Once on the main level, the two headed quickly for the rear of the building and let themselves out the service entrance. It was only 21:00:00—still early for a Saturday night. Nevertheless, Rodney didn't want to take the chance that someone might see them with their travel bags and think it unusual. He peered around the corner at a group of people coming out of Tower 3. In the parking lot across from them, a planetary policeman strolled on Saturday night patrol duty.

"Come on," whispered Rodney, heading the other way.

He and Aurora didn't slow down until they reached the Grand Central Walkway several blocks away. They hopped onto the moving walkway and tried to lose themselves in the crowd.

"We'll find a place to hide until morning," Rodney said. "Somewhere safe and quiet. . . ."

The moving walkway was approaching Recreation Sector, or RecSec, destination of many of the Saturday evening pedestrians. Colorful holographic signs advertised restaurants, entertainment centers, and hotels of all kinds. Rodney saw a small blue sign ahead, not far from the exit ramp, yet away from the hustle and bustle of the main thoroughfare:

Get Away Fr m It All
HOTEL STRATOSPHERE
LOW WEEKLY RAT S

"Come on," he said to Aurora. "We'll get off here." They elbowed their way toward the exit ramp, surrounded by funseekers.

"Oof," said Rodney, as a group of tough-looking young men in black jumpsuits careened onto the ramp and slammed into him. Rodney's bag went flying. One black-suited fellow grabbed it, but Aurora snatched it away, a growl in her throat.

"Well, well," sneered the young man, "a boy and his faithful *Muttus* running away from home, no doubt." He grinned and motioned to his friends, who started to surround the two of them.

"Run for it!" yelled Rodney. He and Aurora jumped off the exit ramp and ran wildly toward the blue sign. They dashed to the left for two blocks, then around to the peeling brick front of the Hotel Stratosphere. They ducked behind the blue glass entrance as the gang rushed past, then doubled back the other way, straight into the arms of—

"*Clutz!*" Rodney threw his arms around the robot.

"Rodney!" cried Clutz, his glassy eyes filled with joy.

"I don't believe it," exclaimed Rodney. He was ecstatic. "I've missed you so much, and I've been so worried about you!"

"I've felt the same about you," said Clutz, "especially these last few minutes. Whatever were you doing?"

"Searching for you," said Rodney, "sector by sector. At least that's what we were going to do. We just had a few problems getting started."

"It would appear so," said Clutz. "Come on. They might come looking for you again." He led Rodney and Aurora back to the Hotel Stratosphere and into the lobby.

"But how did you get here?" asked Rodney. They sat down on a threadbare sofa in one corner. "Tell me everything. Where have you been? How did you find us? Are you all right?"

"Yes, yes, I'm fine," answered Clutz. "A little

the worse for wear, perhaps"—he fingered a dent in the back of his head—"but basically all right.

"I heard the discussion last night, you know. About my having to leave, I mean. I didn't intend to listen, but I couldn't really help it. And when I found out how your parents felt, how I'd failed them as I had failed my previous owners, I decided the right thing was just to end it all. A robot is supposed to help humans, not be a burden to them."

"But you're not—" Rodney cut in.

Clutz held up his hand. "You wanted to hear everything," he said. "So I took the plunge— literally. I jumped down the trash-conveyor chute. I spent most of last night in the main collection bin outside WasteSec, waiting my turn for recycling in the fusion chamber."

"Oh, no," said Rodney. "You can't—"

"Don't worry," said Clutz. "I couldn't. My programming must be a tad short on bravery. Also, the closer I got to that furnace, the more I wanted to see you—and you, of course, Aurora—one more time. If only just to say good-bye.

"So I scrambled over the side, just as the waste bin was about to empty me into the furnace. I singed both heels climbing out. See? I've been riding the moving walkway ever since. I wasn't sure how to get back to your living unit from WasteSec, but I did manage to find the park."

"Then I *did* see you in the reflecting pool this morning," exclaimed Rodney.

"Yes," said Clutz. "But I was afraid to let you know I was there. I was afraid your parents wouldn't want me to see you again, and I didn't want to cause trouble. That's why I was following you in secret. I had to figure out what to do. If those hoodlums hadn't come along just now . . ."

Rodney picked at a worn spot on the sofa. "My mom and dad are thinking of buying a Butler robot," he said. "He's there now."

"Then I guess it's really final," said Clutz with a sigh. "I might as well go back to WasteSec. And you must go home. Your parents will be frantic with worry by now."

"No!" said Rodney. "I'm not letting you go again. I don't care what happens. We'll run away together for real. Or I'll hide you. No one will even know you've come back."

Clutz shook his head sadly. "You can't run away, and I can't stay hidden forever. It wouldn't be the right thing for either of us, even if it's what you want now.

"No," he said, "there are some things that humans as well as robots just have to face up to. We can only take our chances with reality and hope for the best."

Rodney started to sniff. Clutz took his hand and they walked up to the hotel's registration desk.

"May I help you?" asked the lone desk clerk.

"We'd like to use your videophone," said Clutz.

It was almost dawn. The sun was a reddish haze on the windows of the police helijet. Rodney looked out over the gleaming domes of Sector 3.

A new day, he thought to himself. *Please let it be a good one.*

The helijet landed in the parking lot of the John Glenn Living Complex and dropped off its passengers. Rodney, Clutz, and Aurora walked slowly to Tower 3 and into the elevator. Aurora pressed the button for Level 99 with her nose, and they rode up in silence. As they got off the elevator the door of their living unit slid open automatically, but they remained standing outside.

Mr. and Mrs. Pentax rushed to the door.

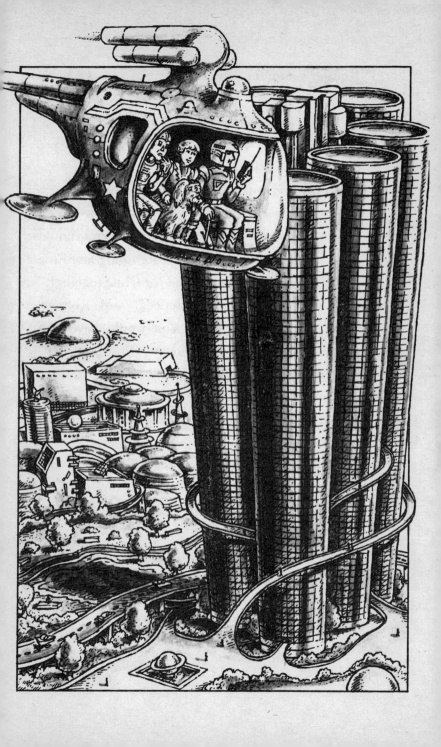

Rodney's mother threw her arms around him. "Thank goodness you're all right," she said.

"We've been out looking for you for hours," said his father. "We even called the police."

Rodney was silent.

"We found your note explaining why you left," his father continued. "Maybe you had to do it, Son, but it wasn't right to worry us so. You should have talked it over with us before doing anything so rash. We could have looked for Clutz together."

"You wouldn't have listened," said Rodney. "You didn't listen before. You would have sent him away again."

Rodney's parents looked at each other and at the robot standing in the doorway next to their son. The boy's hand was held fast in the robot's metal one.

"I didn't want to come back," said Rodney, "but Clutz told me I had to. Please don't ask me to give him up. No Butler robot could ever be what he is."

"Never mind the Butler robot," said Mrs. Pentax with considerable feeling. She moved away from the door so that Rodney could see inside. He gasped. Every piece of furniture and every object in the leisure room had been moved, taken out, or stacked up.

"He was a cleaning freak," said Mrs. Pentax. "He wanted to protect us from germs."

Rodney nodded knowingly.

"He was going to put it all back by morning," said Mrs. Pentax. "But when we found out that he had let you and Aurora run away right under his nose while he was busy chasing dustballs, we couldn't wait to get rid of him. We called Ralph's and told them to come pick him up immediately, even if it was the middle of the night. As far as I'm concerned, the Butler robot was a total failure."

"His cooking was awful, too," said Rodney's father.

"Then he's gone?" asked Rodney.

The Pentaxes nodded and smiled.

"Now, I'm not making any promises," warned Rodney's father. "Another episode like the one with the float-a-lounge and we might have to reconsider. But in light of everything that's happened, and after what you've said—"

"He can stay! You're saying he can stay!"

Rodney dropped his travel bag and hurled himself at his father.

"Oh, Dad, thank you!" He hugged his father until Mr. Pentax thought his neck would break.

Then Rodney turned to Clutz, still standing in the hallway outside the living unit. "Well," he said, smiling, "you heard what my father said. Come on in now. What are you waiting for? You're home."

The robot gazed uncertainly at Rodney, not able to believe what was happening. He took a step forward and tripped over the threshold.

"Nasty step you've got there," he said, straightening his breastplate. Rodney laughed and pulled him inside.

Clutz looked at the familiar walls and at the faces surrounding him. He took the paw Aurora offered and shook it solemnly. Happiness flooded all his circuits.

"Yes," he said at last, "I'm home."

About the Author

Marilyn Z. Wilkes was born and grew up in St. Joseph, Missouri. She received her Bachelor of Arts from Northwestern University and after graduation came east to work as an editor of textbooks in a New York publishing company. Currently Ms. Wilkes lives in Armonk, New York, with her husband and two sons. This is her first book for young readers.

About the Artist

Larry Ross grew up in Lewistown, Pennsylvania, and received his Bachelor of Fine Arts from Pratt Institute in New York. He has previously illustrated books for Doubleday and Harlin Quist, but *C.L.U.T.Z.* is his first science fiction book. Mr. Ross lives in Madison, New Jersey, with his wife and two children.